# THE LEGEND OF
# JOHN HENRY

## BY TERRY SMALL

A Doubleday Book for Young Readers

A Doubleday Book for Young Readers
Published by
Delacorte Press
Bantam Doubleday Dell Publishing Group, Inc.
1540 Broadway
New York, New York 10036
Doubleday and the portrayal of an anchor with a dolphin are trademarks of
Bantam Doubleday Dell Publishing Group, Inc.
Copyright © 1994 by Terry Small

Library of Congress Cataloging in Publication Data
Small, Terry.
    The legend of John Henry / written and illustrated by Terry Small.
       p.  cm.
    Summary: A Herculean steel driver on the railroad pits his strength
and speed against the new steam hammer which is putting men out of
jobs.
    ISBN 0-385-31168-0
    1. John Henry (Legendary character)—Juvenile literature. [1. John
Henry (Legendary character) 2. Folklore—United States. 3. Folklore, Afro-American. 4. Railroads—Folklore.] I. Title.
    PZ8.1.S64Le   1994
    398.2—dc20      91-44928    CIP    AC

Manufactured in Hong Kong
February 1994
10  9  8  7  6  5  3  2  1

In the age-old conflict between man and machine
few heroes stand out like John Henry.
On June 5, 1989, one such man stood alone,
unarmed but defiant, and with nothing but courage and
a determined belief in the rightness of his cause,
stopped a column of army tanks in
Tiananmen Square, Beijing, China.

To him this book is dedicated.

Special thanks to my friends Bernie Garnett and Sheena Stevens,
whose careful considerations and natural instincts
helped impart the ring of truth to these words;
and further acknowledgment to
Kingsley Osondu Okoric.

John Henry, he was born a slave
In a West Virginia shack,
When freedom seemed as far away
As the end of a railroad track.

He growed up big and look so strong,
But sad is all he feel,
And he never smile till he hear the sound
Of a hammer strikin steel.

He watch that driver bustin rock
And his grin begin to grow,
While the shaker hold that rod of steel
On every hammer blow.

When freedom come, John head up north:
"Gon leave this place behin'.
Happiness ain't but a twelve-pound hammer
Ringin this soul of mine."

He work the railroads, drivin steel,
In the days of the Great Expansion,
When a workman live in a company house
And the railroad boss in a mansion.

His shaker Titus hold the rod
While John be drivin it down.
Titus never use tongs; he never trust nothin
But his hands, all knotted and brown.

Ole Titus, he use to be a hammer man, too,
Till he broke his back in the war.
He was fifty-eight years and his strength was gone,
And his hands and his joints was sore.

But nobody brought more heart and will
To the job of holdin the rod.
Most shakers sang to the rhythm of the hammer:
Ole Titus, he sang to God.

They work two years on the Allegheny Line,
Carvin up a rock mountain by hand;
And the railroad spread through the white oak woods
Like a ribbon all cross the land.

Then one fine day a shirtsleeve man,
Josiah Haley by name,
Come into camp with a big machine
And a even bigger claim.

He say to the boss, "This steam drill here
Can put out the work of ten.
Five hundred dollars—cold hard cash—
And you'll never pay a crew again."

By mornin next, the Allegheny Line
Had bought them a Haley Drill;
And they told John Henry and the steel-drivin gang,
"Don't need you no more—never will."

It was a mighty hard blow for some of the men.
Ole Titus, he took it the wu'st.
He laid his ole head on his bundle of clothes,
And they say his ole heart jes bust, Lawd,
   his tired ole heart jes bust.

Then John Henry set out to walkin alone
With his hammer slung over his shoulder,
And he sung him a quiet song to God
For Titus, the steel-rod holder.

And God musta listen mighty hard
To the words John Henry send.
He say to Hisself, "I got me a shaker;
John Henry, he lost him a friend."

Then God come down in a talkin-dream
To the water boy, Li'l Bill:
"Steel-drivin man need a shaker," He say.
"Go hold John Henry's drill."

So Li'l Bill hold while John drive steel
Way up on the North Point Line,
And they cut a straight road through the crooked hills
Of the Seventeen-Mile Incline.

Twelve miles they drove in a handful of months,
But 'fore the first track was laid,
Come the shirtsleeve man with the Haley Drill
On the road John Henry made.

Now it didn't take long for the North Point boss
To take on a steam drill too.
"It'll drive five mile a week," he said,
"And we got no need for you, boys,
     we got no need for you."

Then Li'l Bill step by John Henry's side
Cross the West Virginia line.
"These red shale hills," the big man say,
"They part of this soul of mine.

"A man can leave for the city, they say,
He can leave for to ramble and roam.
But wherever he go, a bit of these hills
Stay wit him, callin him home.

"Long as he move, he gon be pushed,
Till they ain't no place to go—
Time come when a man gotta make a stand
And he ain't gon move no mo'.

"I'm home, Li'l Bill, and I'm home for good;
It's a feelin in my bones and skin.
They ain't no man, ain't no machine
Ever make me leave agin."

Then down from the heights of Cruzee Mountain
A bangin and a clangin rolled:
The sound of the cold steel ring like silver,
Hammers chime like gold.

So big John Henry and his shaker Bill
Took work on the C & O spur:
"Gon teach them boys how to drive some steel
And the boss how to call me 'sir.' "

Then John swing a pair of twenty-pound hammers
With handles of four-foot oak.
By the end of the day the steel was smokin
And the four-foot handles was broke.

Cap'n Tommy was boss of that C & O crew
And a tolerable decent man.
"I like you, John Henry—Lord knows I do—
You does what you says you can."

So month by month that railroad crept
Through the pine-clad virgin hills,
Where crickets sung through the starry nights
To the lonesome whippoorwills;

And daybreak danced to a different tune,
To the *jing-a-ling-ling* of the steel,
And the work crew sang, "It's a brand-new mornin—
Lawd, that's how I feel!
  Good Lawd, that's how I feel!"

Then John laid eyes on a bright young gal
Who smile when she bring him water:
"Don't you know me, John? I Polly Ann—
You ole friend Titus's daughter!"

They loved and married in the months to come,
And a new life jes begin.
Wit Polly Ann, John close to heaven
More'n he ever been.

Then one bright mornin at the company house
Cap'n Tommy standin up at the door,
And he find John Henry stretch out long
In a quilt on the hard wood floor.

"Big John," he say in a serious tone,
"Big John, I got bad news.
There's a man come down, he got a machine,
And me, I gots to choose.

"Don't mean you ain't done right by me,
Li'l Bill and the boys of the crew;
It's jes that progress come to the rails,
And progress don't need you, John—
    progress don't need you."

John Henry rise from the hard wood floor,
Step out in the light of day;
And he stand there starin at the shirtsleeve man
And the steam drill blockin his way.

"Do that machine got a broad ole back,
Big heart, and a callused hand?
Do it move to the rhythm of the ringin steel
And grunt when the hammer land?

"Do it ache and sweat in the blisterin sun,
Do it choke on the dust of stone?
Do that machine got a song to sing
And a soul to call its own?"

"The Haley Drill," said the shirtsleeve man,
"Can put out the work of ten.
Don't need no shakers, water boys,
No cooks, or hammer men.

"It don't need rest, it don't need food,
It don't need housin neither.
Come heat, come cold—the Haley Drill
Ain't bothered much by either.

"And that's the future in your eye—
Get a good look while you can.
Ain't no tomorrow gonna come
For an old steel-drivin man."

John Henry rose hisself up tall,
As tall as he could get.
His shoulders squared as he declared,
"It ain't tomorrow yet.

"Now Mista Haley, move out the way.
This job be needin a man.
Ain't no mountain never stop my hammer;
Don't reckon no steam drill can."

Then the shirtsleeve man say to Cap'n Tommy,
"Like to place me a little bet?
There ain't no uppity, loudmouth boy
Beat the Haley Steam Drill yet.

"I'll stake my machine against his muscle
If you got the mind to agree.
If *I* win, I sell you a Haley Drill;
If *you* win, you get it free."

John Henry jes smile and strip to the waist.
"Well, a man ain't nothin but a man.
But before that steam drill beat me down,
I gon die wit a hammer in my han',
    Lawd, Lawd—gon die wit a hammer in my han'."

So they hauled that machine to the mountainside
And they wedged its wheels on the spot,
And they shoveled in coal through the firebox door
Till the blaze grew shimmerin hot.

Then the water churned in the boiler shell
And the steam hissed through its belly,
And the steel arm clanked and the drill slammed down
And the roadbed shook like jelly.

Cap'n Tommy blew the whistle and the work begun
And the steam drill took off pumpin.
With a furious burst it jumped out first
With the drill rod bump-bump-thumpin.

John Henry, he chose him a twenty-pound hammer;
Li'l Bill, he hold on fast.
The shirtsleeve man say, "Give it up now!
You know it ain't gonna last!"

John Henry, he made the steel drill sing
With the music of the silver bell—
So crisp and clear and light as rain,
Like a dime in a wishin well.

That pure sweet ring jes floatin on air
With the steam and the sweat and the dust,
And it run like a brook through the huffin and puffin
Of the steam drill's boom and bust.

But the rumble and the tumble and the shudder and the crunch
Kept a-thumpin at the hard red shale,
And they heard that shirtsleeve man just a-laughin
How John look mighty frail.

John Henry, he say to his shaker then,
"Got a tightness grabbin my knee.
Quick as I git sweatin, that'll loosen up good—
It'll set my hammer free!"

He swing his arm in a rainbow arc
And the cold steel start to jingle,
And Li'l Bill sing to the rhythm of the ring
Till it make your eardrum tingle.

Then John git to pumpin like a natural man
With his arms all shinin black,
And his legs start swayin to the *ching-a-ling-ding*
With the steam risin off his back.

"Water boy, come here!" John Henry call.
"Git you feets like a rollin wheel!
Bring a bucket for to cool my body down,
Bring another for to cool my steel!"

All day at the Big Bend Tunnel they drove,
John Henry and the Haley Drill,
Till Cap'n Tommy blow the evenin whistle
And the whole mountainside fall still.

When they measure them cuts in the mountain rock
They was cheerin on the C & O Line—
John Henry, he drove some fifteen feet,
And the steam drill jes made nine—Good Lawd!
    The steam drill jes made nine!

But the cheerin of the men was cut by a shriek
Comin out Miz Polly Ann—
And stretch out long on the cold hard ground
Lay a big steel-drivin man.

"Git up!" she cry. "John Henry, git up!"
But big John, he don't git.
He jes lay still with his big eyes watchin
Cap'n Tommy come lickety-split.

"Big John," he say, "don'tcha go nowhere!
You done beat that steam drill down.
Yes sir, yes *sir*! You git on up!
Git up and claim your crown!"

"Gon get me a crown," John Henry say,
"But it ain't gon be down here.
God must be needin some steel drivin done—
He callin right in my ear.

"Come lay my hammer by my side:
I sho' nuff take it along.
Ole Titus, he jes a-waitin up yonder,
Singin him a shaker song."

So they laid John Henry in a hard rock bed
At the edge of the railroad track,
And he ain't gonna leave West Virginia no more,
And he ain't never comin back.

Now the C & O train be thunderin through,
Slowin down at the Big Bend only;
And jes 'fore the tunnel the steam whistle blow,
Singin sad and long and lonely.

Then deep in the mountain where the light don't play
You can listen up the strangest sound—
Like a swingin of the hammer and a ringin of the steel
And a breakin of the hard rock ground.

Then a rumblin noise be rollin on down
Like a shaker singin loud as he can,
And you swear it say as you racin away,
"John Henry was a steel-drivin man, Lawd, Lawd,
    John Henry was a steel-drivin man!"